Discoveries
From Class

selected by Wendy Body

Contents

The Captain's Papers *(Treasure Island)* 2
My Last Home *(Black Beauty)* 10
The Robin Who Showed The Way *(The Secret Garden)* 16
The Open Road *(The Wind in the Willows)* 26
The Terrible Secret *(The Railway Children)* 37

LONGMAN

The Captain's Papers

from *Treasure Island*
by Robert Louis Stevenson (1883)

"What I want to know is this: Supposing that I have here some clue to where Flint buried his treasure, will that treasure amount to much?"

"Amount, sir!" cried the squire. "It will amount to this; if we have the clue you talk about, I fit out a ship in Bristol dock, and take you and Hawkins here along,

and I'll have that treasure if I search a year."

"Very well," said the doctor. "Now, then, if Jim is agreeable, we'll open the packet"; and he laid it before him on the table.

The bundle was sewn together, and the doctor had to get out his instrument-case, and cut the stitches with his medical scissors. It contained two things – a book and a sealed paper.

"First of all we'll try the book," observed the doctor...

"I can't make head or tail of this," said Dr Livesey.

"The thing is as clear as noonday," cried the squire. "This is the black-hearted hound's account-book. These crosses stand for the names of ships or towns that they sank or plundered. The sums are the scoundrel's share, and where he feared an ambiguity, you see he added something clearer. 'Offe

Caraccas'; now, you see, here was some unhappy vessel boarded off that coast. God help the poor souls that manned her – coral long ago."

"Right!" said the doctor. "See what it is to be a traveller. Right! And the amounts increase, you see, as he rose in rank."

There was little else in the volume but a few bearings of places noted in the blank leaves towards the end, and a table for reducing French,

English, and Spanish moneys to a common value.

"Thrifty man!" cried the doctor. "He wasn't the one to be cheated."

"And now," said the squire, "for the other."

The paper had been sealed in several places with a thimble by way of seal; the very thimble, perhaps, that I had found in the captain's pocket. The doctor opened the seals with great care, and there fell out the map of an island, with latitude and longitude, soundings, names of hills, and bays and inlets, and every particular that would be needed to bring a ship to a safe anchorage upon its shores.

It was about nine miles long and five across, shaped, you might say, like a fat dragon standing up, and had two fine land-locked harbours, and a hill in the centre part marked "The Spy-glass". There were several additions of a later date; but, above all, three crosses of red ink – two on the north part of the island, one in the south-west, and beside this last, in the same red ink, and in a small, neat hand, very different from the captain's tottery characters, these words: "Bulk of treasure here."

My Last Home

from *Black Beauty* by Anna Sewell (1877)

In the morning a smart-looking young man came for me; at first he looked pleased, but when he saw my knees, he said in a disappointed voice: "I didn't think, sir, you would have recommended my ladies a blemished horse like that."

"Handsome is – that handsome does," said my master; "you are only taking him on trial, and I am

sure you will do fairly by him, young man, and if he is not as safe as any horse you ever drove, send him back."

I was led home, placed in a comfortable stable, fed and left to myself. The next day, when my groom was cleaning my face, he said: "That is just like the star that Black Beauty had, he is much the same height too; I wonder where he is now."

A little further on he came to the place in my neck where I was bled, and where a little knot was left in the skin. He almost started, and began to look me over carefully, talking to himself.

"White star in the forehead, one white foot on the off side, this little knot just in that place –" then looking at the middle of my back – "and as I am alive, there is that little patch of white hair that John used to call 'Beauty's threepenny bit'. It must be Black Beauty! Why, Beauty! Beauty! do you know me! little Joe

Green, that almost killed you?" And he began patting and patting me as if he was quite overjoyed.

I could not say that I remembered him, for now he was a fine-grown young fellow, with black whiskers and a man's voice, but I was sure he knew me, and that he was Joe Green, and I was very glad. I put my nose up to him, and tried to say that we were friends. I never saw a man so pleased.

The Robin Who Showed The Way

from *The Secret Garden*
by Frances Hodgson Burnett (1911)

Mary skipped round all the gardens and round the orchard, resting every few minutes. At length she went to her own special walk and made up her mind to try if she could skip the whole length of it. It was a good long skip, and she began slowly, but before she had gone half-way down the path she was so

hot and breathless, that she was obliged to stop. She did not mind much, because she had already counted up to thirty. She stopped with a little laugh of pleasure, and there, lo and behold, was the robin swaying on a long branch of ivy. He had followed her, and he greeted her with a chirp. As Mary had skipped towards him she felt something heavy in her pocket strike against her at each jump, and when she saw the robin she laughed again.

"You showed me where the key was yesterday," she said. "You ought to show me the door today; but I don't believe you know!"

The robin flew from his swinging spray of ivy on to the top of the wall and he opened his beak and sang a loud, lovely trill, merely to show off. Nothing in the world is quite as adorably lovely as a robin when he shows off – and they are nearly always doing it.

Mary Lennox had heard a great deal about Magic in her Ayah's stories, and she always said what happened almost at that moment was Magic.

One of the nice little gusts of wind rushed down the walk, and it was a stronger one than the rest. It was strong enough to wave the branches of the trees, and it was more than strong enough to sway the trailing sprays of untrimmed ivy hanging from the wall. Mary had stepped close to the robin, and suddenly the gust of wind swung aside some loose ivy trails, and more suddenly still she jumped towards it and caught it in her hand. This she did because she had seen something under it – a round knob which had been covered by the leaves hanging over it. It was the knob of a door.

She put her hands under the leaves and began to pull and push them aside. Thick as the ivy hung, it nearly all was a loose and swinging curtain, though some had crept over wood and iron. Mary's heart began to thump and her hands to shake a little in her delight and excitement. The robin kept singing and twittering away and tilting his head on one side, as if he were as excited as she was. What was this under her hands which was square and made of iron and which her fingers found a hole in?

It was the lock of the door which had been closed ten years, and she put her hand in her pocket, drew out the key, and found it fitted the keyhole. She put the key in and turned it. It took two hands to do it, but it did turn.

And then she took a long breath and looked behind her up the long walk to see if anyone was coming. No one was coming. No one ever did come, it seemed, and she took another long breath, because she could not help it, and she held back the swinging curtain of ivy and pushed back the door which opened slowly – slowly.

Then she slipped through it, and shut it behind her, and stood with her back against it, looking about her and breathing quite fast with excitement, and wonder, and delight.

She was standing *inside* the secret garden.

The Open Road

from *The Wind in the Willows*
by Kenneth Grahame (1908)

They were strolling along the high road easily, the Mole by the horse's head, talking to him, since the horse had complained that he was being frightfully left out of it, and nobody considered him in the least; the Toad and the Water Rat walking behind the cart talking together – at least Toad was talking, and Rat was saying at intervals, "Yes,

precisely; and what did you say to him?" – and thinking all the time of something very different, when far behind them they heard a faint warning hum, like the drone of a distant bee. Glancing back, they saw a small cloud of dust, with a dark centre of energy, advancing on them at incredible speed, while from out the dust a faint "Poop-poop!" wailed like an uneasy animal in pain. Hardly regarding it, they turned to resume their conversation, when in an instant

(as it seemed) the peaceful scene was changed, and with a blast of wind and a whirl of sound that made them jump for the nearest ditch, it was on them! The "poop-poop" rang with a brazen shout in their ears, they had a moment's glimpse of an interior of glittering plate-glass and rich morocco, and the magnificent motor-car, immense, breath-snatching, passionate, with its pilot tense and hugging his wheel, possessed all earth and air for the fraction of a second, flung an enveloping cloud of dust that blinded and enwrapped them utterly, and then dwindled to a speck in the far distance, changed back into a droning bee once more.

The old grey horse, dreaming, as he plodded along, of his quiet paddock, in a new raw situation such as this simply abandoned himself to his natural emotions. Rearing, plunging, backing steadily, in spite of all the Mole's efforts at his head, and all the

Mole's lively language directed at his better feelings, he drove the cart backwards towards the deep ditch at the side of the road. It wavered an instant – then there was a heartrending crash – and the canary-coloured cart, their pride and their joy, lay on its side in the ditch, an irredeemable wreck.

Toad sat straight down in the middle of the dusty road, his legs stretched out before him, and stared fixedly in the

direction of the disappearing motor-car. He breathed short, his face wore a placid, satisfied expression, and at intervals he faintly murmured “Poop-poop!”

The Mole was busy trying to quiet the horse, which he succeeded in doing after a time. Then he went to look at the cart, on its side in the ditch. It was indeed a sorry sight. Panels and windows smashed, axles hopelessly bent, one wheel off, sardine-tins scattered over the wide world, and the bird in the bird-cage sobbing pitifully and calling to be let out.

The Rat came to help him, but their united efforts were not sufficient to right the cart. “Hi! Toad!” they cried. “Come and bear a hand, can’t you!”

The Toad never answered a word, or budged from his seat in the road; so they went to see what was the matter with him. They found him in a sort of trance, a happy smile on his face, his eyes still fixed on the dusty wake of their destroyer. At intervals he was still heard to murmur "Poop-poop!"

The Rat shook him by the shoulder. "Are you coming to help us, Toad?" he demanded sternly.

"Glorious, stirring sight!" murmured Toad, never offering to move. "The poetry of motion! The *real* way to travel! The *only* way to travel! Here today – in next week tomorrow! Villages skipped, towns and cities jumped – always somebody else's horizon! O bliss! O poop-poop! O my! O my!"

"O *stop* being an ass, Toad!" cried the Mole despairingly.

"And to think I never *knew*!" went on the Toad in a dreamy monotone. "All those wasted years that lie behind me, I never knew ...

The Terrible Secret

from *The Railway Children* by E. Nesbit (1908)

The settle seemed hard and uncomfortable in spite of all the pillows and bolsters and soft folded rugs. It was terrible not to be able to go out. They moved the settle to the window, and from there Peter could see the smoke of the trains winding along the valley. But he could not see the trains.

At first Bobbie found it quite hard to be as nice to him as she wanted to be, for fear he should think her priggish. But that soon wore off, and both she and Phyllis were, as he observed, jolly good sorts. Mother sat with him when the sisters were out. Peter determined not to make any fuss about the pain in his foot, though it was rather bad, especially at night.

There were visitors, too. Mrs Perks came up to ask how he

was, and so did the Station Master, and several of the village people, but the time went slowly, slowly.

"I do wish there was something to read," said Peter, "I've read all our books about fifty times over."

"I'll go to the Doctor's," said Phyllis; "he's sure to have some."

"Only about how to be ill, and about people's nasty insides, I expect," said Peter.

"Perks has a whole heap of

magazines that came out of trains when people are tired of them," said Bobbie. "I'll run down and ask him."

So the girls went their two ways.

Bobbie found Perks busy cleaning lamps.

"And how's the young gent?" said he.

"Better, thanks," said Bobbie, "but he's most frightfully bored. I came to ask if you'd got any magazines you could lend him."

"There, now," said Perks, regretfully, rubbing his ear with a black and oily lump of cotton waste, "why didn't I think of that, now? I was trying to think of something as 'ud amuse him only this morning, and I couldn't think of anything better than a guinea-pig. And a young chap I know's going to fetch that over for him this tea-time."

"How lovely! A real live guinea-pig! He will be pleased. But he'd like the magazines as well."

"That's just it," said Perks. "I've just sent the pick of 'em to Snigson's boy – him what's just getting over the pewmonia. But I've lots of illustrated papers left."

He turned to the pile of papers in the corner and took up a heap six inches thick.

"There!" he said. "I'll just slip a bit of string and a bit of paper round 'em."

He pulled an old newspaper from the pile and spread it on the table, and made a neat parcel of it.

"There," said he, "there's lots of pictures, and if he likes to mess 'em about with his paint-box or coloured chalks or what not, why let him. I don't want 'em."

"You're a dear," said Bobbie, took the parcel, and started. The papers were heavy, and when she had to wait at the level-crossing while a train went by, she rested the parcel on the top of the gate. And idly she looked at the printing on the paper that the parcel was wrapped in.

Suddenly she clutched the parcel tighter and bent her head over it. It seemed like some horrible dream. She read on – the bottom of the column was torn off – she could read no farther.

She never remembered how she got home. But she went on tiptoe to her room and locked the door. Then she undid the parcel and read that printed column again, sitting on the edge of her bed,

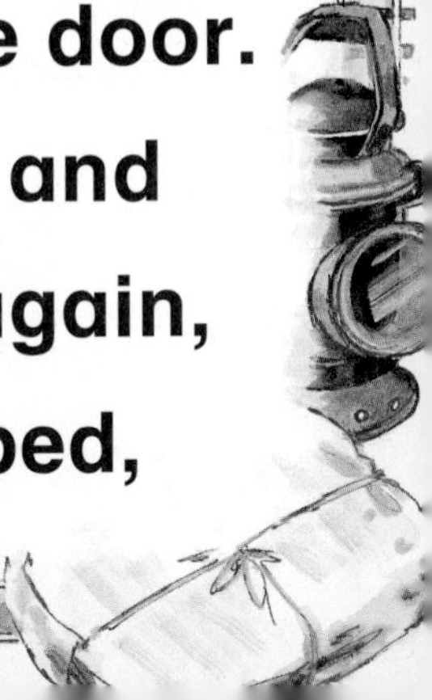

her hands and feet icy cold and her face burning. When she had read all there was, she drew a long, uneven breath.

"So now I know," she said.

What she had read was headed, "End of the Trial. Verdict. Sentence".

The name of the man who had been tried was the name of her father. The verdict was "Guilty", and the sentence was "Five years' Penal Servitude".

"Oh, Daddy," she whispered, crushing the paper hard, "it's not true – I don't believe it. You never did it! Never, never, never!"

There was a hammering at the door.

"What is it?" said Bobbie.

"It's me," said the voice of Phyllis; "tea's ready, and a boy's brought Peter a guinea-pig. Come along down."

And Bobbie had to.